Contents

God's House

MICHÈLE ROBERTS

A Phoenix Paperback

God's House first published in *God* (Serpent's Tail, 1992)
Anger first published in *The Seven Deadly Sins* (Serpent's Tail, 1988)
Both stories taken from *During Mother's Absence* published by Virago,
1993.

This edition published in 1996 by Phoenix
a division of Orion Books Ltd
Orion House, 5 Upper St Martin's Lane, London WC2H 9EA

ISBN 1 85799 761 1

Typeset by Deltatype Ltd, Ellesmere Port, Cheshire
Printed in Great Britain by Clays Ltd, St Ives plc

Anger

Once upon a time, there was a red-haired country-woman called Bertrande living with her husband, Guillaume Tarentin, in their small house tucked into the side of a steep hill in Provence. Further down the pebbly track which led as far as their stone porch and nowhere else was a small orchard of apple and apricot trees, and, beyond that, quite a way down, two or three other small houses in which their neighbours lived. Right at the bottom of the hill was the village itself. Guillaume always said he liked living so high up, on account of the peace and quiet. The neighbours said it was so Bertrande could shout at him without anybody hearing. The neighbours added that Bertrande also liked being able to look down her big nose at everyone else.

This was literally true. When she hung the washing out in the mornings, the neighbours, if they craned their necks, could see her look up at the vast sky over her head, gaze at the hillside sheering on up above her, and then stare down at the roofs of their own houses. She had an odd rigid posture always, and at these moments would wrap her fists in her apron. Then up on tiptoe she would go, still staring down at them, until you would have thought her legs and feet must be made of wood.

Guillaume was well-off by village standards. He and Bertrande could afford to eat their own produce, once the landlord had taken his share, not just sell it all and subsist on bread and root vegetables as the very poorest did. They ate eggs from their own chickens, and killed and boiled the same fowls when these got too old for laying; they could afford to buy olive oil to dip their bread into; if they only ate roast meat on big feast days well at least they could afford bones for soup; and Bertrande, like all the women of the village, was skilled at stretching a little a long way. What was left over from one day got turned into something else the next. Likewise, she had the knack of making clothes and utensils out of odd materials. The ticking that covered her goose-feather quilts served also to make shirts and chemises for herself and her husband; earthenware flowerpots held her wooden spoons and spatulas and tin ladles; she cut up bits of old felt to make slippers and boots. She saved everything, and found a use for it. Bits of string, knotted together, mended chair seats and baskets; she grew flowers in old saucepans, which she then stuck in a row on the windowsill; out of old boxes she made cupboards and stools; out of old cardboard she made patches for broken windows, mats for the kitchen floor of trodden earth, trays on which to store vegetables.

Thrift and good housekeeping were all very well, the neighbours thought, but Bertrande went too far. She was seen at Mass with chicken feathers, not ribbons, stuck in her shawl for decoration. The holy water stoup hung from a nail in the kitchen held salt. Surely her cheeks were sometimes redder than nature intended? Why, even in summer, did she swaddle herself in long heavy clothes, and shiver? Why, when she came down to the village once a week for market, was she sometimes heard singing songs that no one else knew? Sometimes she did not come down at all, and it was Guillaume who had to take her place, with his heavy baskets of fruit and vegetables, amongst the other women. Kindly, they looked away from him, and only shrugged to one another. They knew that when Bertrande should have been about her work in house and garden she was sometimes to be seen wandering on the hillside collecting wild flowers. Not to dry them for tisanes, oh no; she pressed them, stuck them on squares of sugar paper, and hung them on the wall. They felt sorry for her husband and were not surprised when after the market packed up he would vanish into the dark little village bar and get roaring drunk before staggering back up the hill.

Bertrande's hands were the largest of any woman's in the village, broad and red, marked with chilblains in winter, seamed with dirt in spring, often puckered with scars and scorch blisters, for she was clumsy in her work much of the time, didn't seem to learn from mistakes. Her hands were capable though, when they wanted to be. When it was a question of money. Her hands could gesture well when she wanted to drive a hard bargain over the price of her fat sweet tomatoes; her hands could seize and wring a goose's neck in seconds; her hands could force open a goose's stubborn beak and stuff it with grain to fatten it well; her hands could slaughter ducks and butcher lambs; her thick fingers could sort coins into shining piles of silver in a twinkling. But what you never saw Bertrande's hands doing was caressing a child. Married for ten years, she appeared incapable of conceiving an heir.

The neighbours pitied Bertrande for this calamity. They conceded the pride that would not let her discuss it, even while they deplored it. They were ready to offer suggestions and remedies, but Bertrande refused to talk about it. She hardly spoke to them at all. This was odder than ever, the neighbours thought, when you considered that Bertrande was well known, in other ways, to be a noisy woman. She suffered from bad dreams at night, they knew, for she often woke her neighbours with her yells. They could hear her nag her husband when he came home drunk; her screams carried down the hillside. She quarrelled with Guillaume frequently for no good reason; the neighbours, pruning their apple trees or digging their vegetable plots, could hear her cursing him in her guttural voice. They were used to the racket she made.

So when at last she fell pregnant, and turned even more sullen and quiet with them, the village women were not so much relieved as worried. They hadn't noticed her belly swelling for a good few months, hidden as it was under her heavy black clothes. When they did, and joked with her about it, she flinched away, grumbling. She wouldn't accept offers of help and advice from the other women, who were hurt by this. At last they could welcome her as one of themselves, yet she snubbed every attempt at friendliness. Once, the midwife, meeting her in the little cemetery next to the church, reached out and patted Bertrande's belly, and the younger woman turned on her and hissed.

Everyone knew, of course, that Bertrande had come to live with her husband from a far-off village, right over the other side of the hill. So they were prepared to make certain allowances for a stranger, and indeed, they always had. And pregnant women were known to behave oddly, to have strange fancies, to crave strange foods. But this behaviour was too proud and angry to pass unnoticed. So the anxious village women began to watch her even more closely.

In her fifth month of pregnancy, Bertrande was spotted in the woods digging up certain roots that were well known to bring on young women's monthly flows, and indeed were prescribed by the midwife for just this reason. In her sixth month of pregnancy, Bertrande was observed helping her husband in their upper field to clear it of rocks and boulders preparatory to ploughing: she picked up the heaviest possible rocks and lugged them to the edge of the hill, where it sheered off into a steep cliff, and tipped them over one by one, grunting like a pig with the effort. That Sunday, after Mass, the priest remonstrated with Guillaume. He should not let his wife roam so far from home into the woods to collect roots that could do her harm if she ate them. He

5

should not have decided to clear the upper field, at last, at just this time. Certainly his wife's labour was essential to his making a living, no one would dispute that, but still, there were limits that should not be passed. Guillaume listened, and sighed. Then he beckoned his wife over from where she stood grumpy and silent among the other women, and took her back up the hill. That night, for the first time since the young couple had come to live there, the neighbours heard the sound of sobbing coming from Guillaume's house.

In her seventh and eighth months, Bertrande seemed calmer. She still spoke little, but she went about her usual work with her old doggedness, and was even heard once or twice singing some of her peculiar songs. But in the lulls at market, when customers were few and there was a chance to gossip and relax, she did not occupy herself stitching clothes for the baby. What are you going to wrap it in? the other women asked her: one of those old sacks you're so fond of making cushions out of? a piece of cardboard? Bertrande threw her arms in the air and laughed loudly, and a kitchen knife fell out of her sleeve and clattered on the cobblestones under the market stall.

The baby came two weeks early, on midwinter night. The midwife, sweating up the hill through the deep snow, got to the house to find two of the neighbours sitting with the labouring woman, one on each side of her big bed, and their husbands offering Guillaume tots of potato brandy in the kitchen below. Each time his wife cried out, Guillaume drank another glass of brandy. Tears ran out of the corners of his red-rimmed eyes, and he crashed his fists on to the tabletop in time to the rhythm of the shouts from above. The midwife bathed Bertrande's face, and encouraged her. Outside, the snow fell. The men stoked the fire in the kitchen, and crouched over it, hating that room above and the pain in it. They kicked the dogs who whined to get closer to the warm red flames, and they played cards, and drank potato brandy until they fell asleep and did not have to listen any more. The newborn's thin wail interrupted their dreams of suffering, and they woke, and looked at each other blearily, then got up clumsily and knelt down on the cold mud floor and thanked God.

Guillaume went shyly upstairs to see his son. The son, however, was a daughter.

– Never mind, his two friends consoled him when he came back downstairs: better luck next time. We'll drink her health anyway.

The midwife, who was like most of the others a kind woman when she could afford to be, came every day to see Bertrande and the child, as did the two neighbours, who made pots of lentil soup and cleaned the house and kept the fire going while the three men dug paths through the snow to the stables and saw after the animals. The women clucked and shook their heads over Bertrande's housekeeping arrangements. Never before, they remonstrated with each other, had they known such a slut, one who kept a stack of wax crayons and a drawing-book in her larder, whose linen chest contained a litter of chestnuts and corks and dried berries threaded on strings, who had decorated the wall behind the privy with her own finger and palm prints, and who had hidden a pack of Tarot cards at the bottom of the flour bin. Still, they were so happy running their fingers through worn patches in the best towels, and examining the top of the high mantelpiece for dust, and wondering whether the inky scrawls on bits of paper stuffing the draughty gaps in the windows were spells or illicit love letters, that when they went up to the bedroom to check how the new mother was doing they were in a cheerful frame of mind and could be patient with her.

For Bertrande found it very difficult to feed her baby. Indeed, the women whispered, you could say she didn't want to. She needed a lot of encouragement to do it, and it seemed that even when she did her milk was thin and did not adequately nourish the baby, who cried a lot in a fretful sort of way that was hard to bear. Still, the baby, who at first had seemed weak and sickly, was at least surviving. In no time at all, the women counselled Bertrande, in a couple of days, say, the little one would take to the breast without such fuss, and then the milk would flow more easily and Bertrande would relax and all would be well.

The crying drove Guillaume from the house, you could see that. He could be of little use, of course, for the women were there with his wife doing everything, and it was not a man's place anyway. He took to neglecting even the jobs he could have been doing in that bad weather, bits of mending and glueing and general re-fixing, and the house grew even more tumbledown around him. He did the bare minimum for the animals, then slouched out, saying he was going down to the neighbours to see if they needed him for anything. The two husbands reported that they never saw him. It was clear that he slipped and slithered down the snowy path to the village bar most evenings, for he would return just as the two women were about to leave for their own homes, wet through and smelling of brandy. He was suffering, but no one could ask him why, for that was not their way. No one had words for what was going on, and they never had had. The priest might have had words for it, but he never came up the hill in the bad weather, and the women did not dare suggest that Guillaume go and visit him. They watched Bertrande turn her head away when her husband came into the bedroom and hovered by the cradle, they saw her look contemptuously at him as he slunk out, they saw her mouth set hard and her big red hands make lumpy fists under the sheet. She wouldn't say the rosary with them of an evening. She wouldn't let them touch the baby with holy water in case the devil carried its soul away before they got it down to the church for a christening. Yet it was well known that these practices were efficacious. The women sighed. With such a mother, what prospect was there for the child?

After a week, there came a thaw. The two husbands took it as a signal to call their wives home, where they were much needed, and the midwife departed to a nearby village to attend another lying-in.

Bertrande and Guillaume were left alone with each other and the baby.

When the thing happened, it took a while for the villagers to make sense of it. As the neighbours explained to the people living lower down the hill, Guillaume was in such a state of anxiety when he came sliding down the muddy track to their door that for a while they could get nothing out of him, only curses and weeping. They gave him brandy, and that steadied him. Then he told them. But even then he was so incoherent and muddled that his worried listeners had to piece his story together for themselves, and, once the news had flown down the hill and began to be passed round the village, no one could be quite sure of the right order of Guillaume's words any more, let alone what had actually happened.

Guillaume said the fire was out. No, Bertrande said that the fire was out. She was cold, and so was the baby. She needed fire. She needed to be warm. She wanted to go back to bed, not to sit in a cold kitchen with no fire. Guillaume went out to the shed to fetch wood for the fire. The fire was not out. The fire was near Bertrande. Bertrande was near the fire. She made more fire with the poker. The flames licked up. She held the baby to the fire to make it warm, like the fire inside her. She held the fire to the baby. Bertrande dropped the baby in the fire. She said it was not an accident.

Later, the priest tried to sort out the right words. Bertrande. The baby fell in the fire by accident.

But everyone knew that that was not really true. And the

priest was not there so how could he know? And Bertrande was never seen in church again, so it was clear she had not made her confession: he had not found out that way.

The child lived. Miraculously, the women said, crossing themselves, her little face was unscathed when Guillaume picked her off the glowing embers and tore the smouldering wrappings off. Though she had been dropped face downwards, only the skin on the uppermost part of her body had been touched by the red ashes burning through. Though the new skin would grow again, it would be shiny and angry and red. But she would not die.

The priest came puffing up the hill to christen the child. They named her Melusine. No one knew where the name came from, and no one dared ask. Guillaume simply said that it would be so. Bertrande went to bed and stayed there and was silent. They brought the child to her to be fed, and they watched her to make sure that she did not try to harm it again. Downstairs in the kitchen, drinking unhappy toasts to the bandaged newborn, they whispered to each other that Bertrande was a monster.

After that, the midwife sent for her sister, who was unmarried, to come and keep house for Guillaume and to keep an eye on Bertrande, who remained in bed and would not get up. Nor would she speak to anyone. Luckily, the midwife's sister was a cheerful girl, who was not affected by the atmosphere in the house. She did not mind drunken men, being used to them, and when one night, on returning from the village bar, Guillaume pulled open the front of her blouse, she only giggled a bit. She told her sister all about it, and her sister told her to be careful. People would talk.

Betrande would not talk. She heard the whisperings, the women knew, which sidled up through the floorboards, down the chimney, in at the window: they did not always bother to lower their voices. It was right she should know what they thought.

They always said the same thing. They watched the words settle inside her, souring her stomach so that she could not eat or drink. They watched the words gnaw at her soul, worrying at it, shredding it to rags and holes. They watched her feed what was left of her soul into her daughter's rosy mouth which ardently sucked it in. The baby seemed to use up her mother's strength: she flourished, while Bertrande grew weaker day by day. Or perhaps, the women whispered, the devil was claiming his own. You could see how Bertrande did not resist him; she drifted easily towards her death. Guillaume slept in the kitchen now. One morning, awakened early by the baby's cries, he stumbled upstairs to rouse his wife to feed her, and found Bertrande cold and stiff against the big square pillow. Her hair, he told the neighbours later, was unplaited and loose all round her face, and there was a thick strand of it caught between her lips.

The priest decided that since Bertrande had not been arraigned and convicted of any crime, charity dictated that she be buried in the corner of the churchyard, close enough to the church to be included in the company of the righteous, and at a sufficient distance not to cause offence. It was a poor funeral, people said afterwards: like a pauper's. They understood why Guillaume would not allow any flowers, and why he did not invite them back to his house afterwards, and why he marked the grave with a plain cross made of cheap wood with no words cut on it other than his wife's name. What else could he have done? Bunched in their best black, separated from him by six feet of respect, they watched him stand, pale and dry-eyed, at the grave's edge, while the priest read out the words of prayers that were snatched from his mouth by the wind and soon lost.

Then Guillaume needed a new wife. He needed her hands labouring in the kitchen and the fields and the garden, he needed her broad back to help him bear his sorrow and shame, he needed her cunt in his bed at night. He needed her eyes never to look into his in the way that Bertrande's had. So, since his friends and the priest went on at him that he should regularise the position in which the midwife's sister found herself, he seduced her properly and then married her. Everybody agreed it was for the best. The wet-nurse jiggled Melusine up and down in her arms, and the plump red-haired baby laughed with pleasure.

Melusine must always have known, Pierre Caillou thought, the story of her mother's life and death. It must have grown her, have shaped her. But it was not this old scandal that made him notice her particularly: he grew interested in

Melusine only when he first realised she had a secret.

Pierre Caillou was the village schoolmaster. He was an educated man, who had left the village to study fifty kilometres away in the great city none of his compatriots had ever seen, and who had returned full of ideas and compassion, determined to give his neighbours' children the chance to learn how to read and write and to lead better lives than those of their parents. After five years of trying to run an elementary school on proper scientific lines, he admitted defeat, acquired a stooped back, and contented himself with teaching those children whose parents let them attend school when they were not needed in the fields or in the house. He had a lot of free time, with so few scholars. So he became himself a student again, first of local folklore and superstition, and then, more precisely, of the customs, morals and beliefs of his fellow villagers. They resented him for this, and he did not blame them. He knew he was privileged, doing no physical work, and with his schoolmaster's stipend topped up by the rents from two farms he had inherited from his parents. He had no friends, though he occasionally played backgammon with the priest on those nights when loneliness drove him to accept the old curé's stupid tolerance of his atheism. He slept at the school, on a truckle bed set up in his office. At night he would extinguish the fire, bundle himself in a grey woollen blanket, and scribble in his notebook. He had a row of these on the mantelpiece, all identical, cheap flimsy notebooks

bound in brown cloth.

At fourteen years old, Melusine was still coming to school each morning. It kept her out of mischief, Guillaume said to Pierre, shrugging his shoulders, it kept her from getting in the way, and if she picked up some useful knowledge, well, all to the good. She could do his accounts for him and prove her usefulness that way. Madame Tarentin agreed: these days, people needed a bit of booklearning. And Melusine already knew most of what there was to know about tending a house. She could afford to put in some time at school. She could help her parents in the afternoons, when the school was closed.

Melusine always sat in the corner of the classroom, near the black iron stove, the best place because the warmest, which she had won on account of being the oldest scholar, and a position she defended with kicks and biting when necessary. Yet she also liked it, Pierre Caillou thought, because the angle of the wall and the bulge of the stove cut her off from the other children, and because she could look out of the window beside her at the short row of pollarded limes edging the path up to the church and watch the comings and goings of people and animals and birds. She daydreamed a lot, and he often had to reprove her, for her inattention was an affront to his authority over the other children. Yet she was a good student: she could read and write well, unlike most of the others, and she was quick at sums when she put her mind to it.

One day he spied on her from behind, peering over her shoulder before she could run the sponge over her slate. He had set the children a geography test, commanding them to draw a map of their province complete with rivers and towns. But Melusine had chosen to sketch, in her coloured chalks, the portrait of some mythical creature she must have seen in a picturebook somewhere: a wild being of the woods, half-man, half-beast, covered from head to toe in thick curly fur, and with little breasts peeping out that proved her to be female.

– What's this? Pierre Caillou asked, reaching his hand over Melusine's shoulder and grabbing her slate.

He moved round in front of her in order to see her face. It was dreamy and contented; she was still in her daydream, her pleasure. He realised that she was not as ugly as he had always thought. It was when she was afraid that she grew ugliness as an extra and protective skin. Still absorbed in her drawing, still attached to it, she was soft, shining.

– Where did you copy this from? he persisted: where did you find it?

Melusine hesitated.

– Nowhere, she said: I just drew it.

He reached for the sponge. She watched him. She was impassive, hard again. He touched the sponge to the slate. Her face twitched.

– In the mirror, she blurted: I saw it in the mirror.

– Stay behind at twelve o'clock, he commanded: I want to get to the bottom of this.

It was cold in the little office where he slept. Melusine stood by the open door, shivering. Noticing, he gestured her in, shut the door behind her, and lit the fire. Normally he never permitted himself a fire in the morning. Only ever at night.

He sat on the truckle bed and she stood in front of him where he ordered her to stand.

– Take your clothes off, he said: show me.

Melusine frowned.

– Don't be silly, he scolded: I am your teacher, there can be nothing wrong. Do as I tell you.

She stood, stiff, between his knees. So he undressed her himself, laying her black school overall carefully on the bed beside him, undoing the buttons of her smock one by one, tugging the rough linen chemise over her head, till he had her naked to the waist.

He knew, of course, as did everyone in the village, that she had been burnt as a baby, and that the midwife had said that the skin would grow back but would be shiny and puckered and red, that she would be grotesque in the place where the women of that country were smooth milky white. What he had not expected were the little breasts. He had thought her too young. What he had not expected was the thick, silky thatch of bright red hair that curled from her neck down around her breasts and on down to her waist.

He stretched his hand out. It shook a little. He touched the red mat of hair, and then her breasts, first one and then the other. Melusine tried to step backwards and he gripped her between his knees.

– Don't be frightened, he told her: I won't hurt you.

He suddenly found that he wanted her to want his caresses. He had never touched a woman before. He wanted her to unbend towards him, as though he were the fire and she could warm herself at him.

– Melusine, he demanded: when did this happen?

She hung her head and mumbled. Even when he laid her gently on the bed and lifted up her skirts, she said nothing he could understand.

– I'll take you home, he decided afterwards: I must speak to your father about this.

The Tarentins were obliged to ask him in to share their midday meal. All the time he was reaching for more bread, or accepting a second plate of cabbage soup, or wiping his greasy mouth on the back of his hand, he was watching Melusine, who sat at the far end of the table and of course said nothing. In those days children did not speak in front of their elders, and Pierre Caillou approved of this. It allowed him to speak of Melusine as though she were not there. His questions, however, alarmed Madame Tarentin, and she sent her stepdaughter outside to sweep the yard. For a moment he saw Melusine's moon face glimmer sadly at the little window; then her father shook his fist at the glass and she disappeared.

Some months before, the parents told him, Melusine was discovered scrubbing herself under the pump, trying to get rid of the unsightly growth of hair that had appeared overnight on the scarred skin of her chest. At the same time they had not only caught her rootling in the old wooden chest into which Bertrande's things had been thrown after her death, but had discovered that she had used the stubs of wax crayon she found there to produce drawings of a hideous sort. No amount of beatings administered by her worried father could stop her drawing. No amount of herbal poultices applied by her worried stepmother could get rid of the thick growth of hair. In the end they used Guillaume's cut-throat razor and shaved it off. But the hair had simply grown back the next month, and she had gone on making her drawings on every scrap of cardboard she could lay her hands on. The most disturbing aspect of the whole business, the parents admitted, was that the hair regularly disappeared of its own accord after four or five days, and reappeared with equal regularity a month later. Bertrande, that unhappy woman, and here they both crossed themselves, had delivered herself of a monster.

Pierre Caillou and Melusine were married soon afterwards, just as soon as the banns had been properly read and Melusine had finished hemming the last sheet and nightgown in her trousseau which, like all the girls in the village, she had started sewing at an early age. She didn't bring Pierre Caillou much, for her parents had little money to spare that winter, and he used this fact to put pressure on them to agree to the marriage. They were relieved, he could see, to get their daughter settled with the only man in the village who could possibly have accepted her.

– Now she's got you to look after her, Madame Tarentin told him: she'll be all right at last. I shan't have to worry about what will become of her any more.

– It's right she should marry and go with you, Guillaume said: poor thing.

They made only one condition. Pierre must promise never to look at his wife unclothed during the period each month when the hair grew on her chest and around her breasts, for this would shame her too much and so halt her chances of living some sort of normal married life. And perhaps, Madame Tarentin added, if he allowed her at those times of seclusion to do the drawing and painting she so loved, she would grow reconciled to her deformity and fret about it less.

For several months Pierre Caillou was happy with his new wife. She spoke little, it was true, but he was used to silence, having lived alone for so long, and found her taciturnity a relief rather than a problem. Her stepmother had trained Melusine well: she could cook, sew and clean quite adequately, and she did not complain about the cold and the draughts in the disused classroom they began to use as a bedroom, nor did she nag him for more housekeeping or new clothes. He was able to go on living much as he always had; she did not grudge him the books he sent for from the bookshops in the city, nor the pipes of tobacco he smoked at night when writing up his notes. He knew that she needed greatly to please him, to show her gratitude that he had taken her on, and he argued with himself that this was quite right, for had he not rescued her from a life of miserable loneliness? The villagers might gossip about them for a while, might indulge their curiosity about the new ménage for as long as it took them to become bored with the young couple's obvious blamelessness and contentment, but in time the whispers and sniggers would die down. His neighbours had not, he knew, expected him to marry. He took a certain pleasure in walking with Melusine on Sunday afternoons up and down the village street, and watching the looks cast at his wife's freshly ironed Sunday gown, at her neat coil of red hair under her bonnet, at the scrubbed pair of sabots she kept for best, at her large blue eyes demurely cast down and her wide mouth firmly closed over her sharp little teeth. She was as comely, on these occasions, as any other girl in the village, and he prided himself on the fact that she was also far more intelligent.

He taught her to keep a certain distance. He would not allow her to attend Sunday Mass, for he wanted to wean her from superstition and bigotry, and he did not allow her to climb the hill to visit her parents more than once every two months, for he wanted to give her a chance to lead her own life and become independent of peasant ways. At night she practised reading, writing and spelling under his supervision, and she soon proved herself skilled enough to take dictation, when he needed to think aloud, and to make fair copies into manuscript from his notebooks. Nor did he forget his promise to her parents: when the hair around her breasts came each month he sent her to sleep on his old truckle bed which was set up at these times in the pantry beyond the kitchen at the back of the schoolroom. He let her keep her paints and paper there and retire early, on what he called her red nights, to mess about to her heart's content with water and colours by the light of a tallow candle. After five nights of sleeping separately, she would return, docile and quiet, to his bed, and to any caresses he felt like making. When he asked to see her paintings she looked cross and shook her head at first, but when he threatened to enter her sanctum and fetch them himself she instantly complied. He was surprised at how well this untaught peasant girl could paint, and praised her unstintingly. He spoke to her of the art galleries in the cities he had visited in his days as a student, and her eyes gleamed as she listened. He sent for volumes of engravings, and explained composition to her, and she smiled her rare smile. He knew that he was ignorant of love in the way that his fellow students had practised it, for he had been much too shy to visit brothels with them. He knew that he was ignorant of love in the way that the men in the village practised it, for he suspected them of being animals who treated their wives as holes in the ground to be pissed into and made pregnant year after year. Melusine suited him, for she needed him and looked up to him. So as well as studying her peculiarities be began to love her, and to hope that she loved him in return.

He began to look forward to the evening, to the clock on the mantelpiece chiming seven-thirty, the hour at which he cleared his books off the table and Melusine in her stout calico apron came in to lay the cloth and then brought in the steaming tureen of delicious soup. Afterwards, as she sat sewing in the chair opposite his, or perched next to him at the table and copied out notes under his direction, he would look at her big forehead, her capable square-tipped fingers, her downcast eyes, and want her to look back at him. He began to want to know what went on in her mind.

But she would not respond in the way he wanted. Where he hoped for naïve confidences, for the revelations of her fresh young heart, he got stories she had picked up from her parents as a child, or details of recipes, or gossip overheard on their Sunday walks together. Melusine, it appeared, was not so very different from the other women in the village after all. She was not, after all, original. She told him nothing he could not have heard himself at the baker's or the butcher's or the bar. Even at night, when he lay in her arms after they had made love in the way he liked best, he could not catch her off-guard. She would say she was sleepy, turn over, and hide her eyes from him.

So he began to think about her secret again. It was here, he concluded, that the core of her personality lay. Hadn't he always known that, right from that first day when he caught her drawing in the classroom? So he began to question her, timidly at first and then with growing confidence, about how she felt about the thick growth of hair that came and went every month around her breasts, about how she felt about the stories concerning her mother that were still rife in the village, about how she felt on those nights when she sat in the pantry by the light of her tallow candle and painted the pictures she saw inside herself. Wasn't he right that there were some paintings she never showed him, that she kept secret? But Melusine just looked at him blankly, and shrugged. Or she would kiss him, to quieten him that way. Or, if they were in bed together, she would begin to fondle him in the expert way she had developed. He began to wish she had not learned so well how to please him. Yet he liked being pleased by her, and the more he liked it the more he grew desperate to be sure she loved him and was not just doing her duty.

But the more he pestered her to talk about her secret feelings and thoughts, the more he begged her to show him *all* her paintings, the more Melusine grew silent, irritable and finally rebellious. She said *no* frequently. She kept the key of the pantry door in her pocket. And at the same time he was forced to notice that not only had she developed the habit of littering the kitchen and their bedroom with pictures and drawings and rough sketches, she had also begun to spend more nights shut away from him each month. Five nights at first, then six, then seven, then eight. And the villagers, who liked to pop in and out of the school and see how Melusine and Pierre were getting on, began to notice that Melusine was turning out as undomestic as her mother had been. The villagers began to whisper and giggle about a husband who could not control his eccentric wife. Pierre Caillou, who had always insisted that he didn't care a damn about gossip, began to suffer.

Some days Melusine was late cooking supper, and held a

sketch in one hand while she served crisp fried potatoes with the other. Sometimes, on a Sunday, she neglected to put on her pretty clothes and complained she didn't want to take a walk with her husband, she'd rather stay indoors and draw. Often at night now she made love to him in such a brisk perfunctory fashion that he felt used, and that she was rushing the love-making so as to be done with it and sleep.

When, one month, Melusine returned to his bed after nine nights in the pantry, Pierre enquired whether the cause of her strange behaviour were perhaps that she were pregnant? Melusine laughed: no. Was she ill? Would she see the doctor? No.

He wondered whether she had taken a lover in secret, whether she lay in the pantry with some red-faced peasant and cuckolded him month and after month. No, Melusine said. Laughing at him before she turned away to swill a plate covered with dried smears of blue and green paint.

He started staying awake at night, so that he could stare at her as she slept, and try to wrest her secret from her closed eyelids or the low words she sometimes muttered as she dreamed. He followed her about the house as she expertly swept and scrubbed, watching the stoop of her broad back, the dexterity of her wrists. He tried to trick her in the evenings, shooting sudden questions at her. He examined the chest where she kept her clothes mixed up with a rubbish of dried flowers and chicken feathers and withered chestnuts. He grew thin with worry, and sometimes forgot to shave in the mornings. He knew he was behaving strangely, and was frightened because he had no control over himself any more. He told Melusine more and more often how much he loved her, but all she would do was pat him on the arm or cuddle him as though he were a child seeking reassurance and then turn away to her housework or her drawing.

On the tenth night of the following month, Melusine had still not returned to his bed. He lay shaking under the grey woollen blankets, and tried to put his worry outside himself so that he could see it and name it and conquer it. Then he realised that he wasn't simply jealous about his wife's passion for spending increasing amounts of time away from him locked in the pantry getting up to unknown mischief. No. He was deeply concerned for her health and well-being. Here the fear leapt up and growled at him. His whole body trembled, but he forced himself to go on thinking. If the hair around Melusine's breasts were staying on her body for a longer time each month, did that not logically suggest that there would come a time when his wife would be disfigured by the hair *every* day of *every* month? And supposing the hair went on growing until it had completely covered her body? Had he married a real wild woman of the woods, half-human and half-beast, of the sort the villagers, whispered about when telling tales around their fires at night? *Was* she truly a monster, as her parents had hinted?

He leapt up, dragged on his dressing-gown and shoved on his slippers, and went to his office, to the rows of books on his shelves dealing with myth, with anthropology, with fairy stories. With metamorphosis and changelings and werewolves. His fingers ran from index to index, from tome to tome. And he read right through all the notebooks in which for so many years now he had carefully recorded all the superstitions and folkloric customs of the primitive people he lived among.

He lifted his head, surprised by a change in the light. His tallow candle was burning low, and a grey glimmer in the dark sky met his eyes when he pushed open the shutters of the window and leaned out to gulp in the sweet, cold night air. It would soon be dawn. It would soon be breakfast time. Soon, his wife would serenely emerge from her hiding-place and rake out the stove before laying and lighting a fire and boiling a pan of water for coffee.

He walked into the kitchen, and saw that a gold crack of light showed under the pantry door. Then he knew what he had to do. It was very simple. He told himself he was not breaking his promise to Melusine's parents. Things had gone too far for worrying about keeping promises. He had a right to know what his wife got up to night after night on her own in there. He had a right to know whether her chest was still covered with hair after ten nights of seclusion. He had a right to know whether he had unwittingly married a monster.

So he banged on the door. Silence. He rattled the door-knob. Silence. Trying to open the door, he found it was indeed locked. So he knelt down and peered in through the keyhole.

The pantry was ablaze with light. Standing in the centre of the tiny room, leaning one hand on the table, was the most beautiful woman Pierre had ever seen. She was naked. She was tall, and creamy skinned, and her long red hair flowed down her back like streams of fire. There was no blemish anywhere on her. She turned her head and smiled at someone he could not see, someone standing just outside his line of vision. Her lips moved, and she spoke. He could not hear her words, nor could he, squinting, make out their shape by lip-reading. Then she turned her head and looked straight at the door.

He roused the neighbours with his screams. When finally they broke the pantry door down, the candles had been blown out, leaving only the harsh smell of tallow, and there was no one in the room. All Melusine's painting equipment had vanished. On the table there lay only a bundle of red-stained rags.

The footprints in the earth of the flowerbed under the school's pantry window could also be traced in the muddy ruts of the village street. Some people said they stopped at the fishpond. Others said they led towards the river. Still others said they went towards the disused well beside the church. No one could be sure.

As the news of Melusine's disappearance spread, reports began to come in from neighbouring villages, brought by men and women who had never met her and knew her only as the daughter of Bertrande.

There was a red-haired woman patient in the lunatic asylum at St Rémy. A red-haired woman had been seen boarding the train for Aix. A red-haired prostitute in Marseilles had recently aborted a son with two heads. The painters down from Paris for the summer at Oppède-le-Vieux had a red-haired woman amongst them. There was a red-haired monster lady in the freak show travelling the coast.

None of the villagers could imagine where Melusine had gone.

Dead people go to Purgatory, to have all the badness burnt out of them by a great fire. But the fire happens when you are born, not after you are dead.

We love each other so much. You hold me in your arms, you kiss my breasts, here, here, then you kiss my belly and in between my legs. We will always be faithful to each other. I will hold your hand palm down on the top of the stove until you swear never to leave me.

I kiss and lick all of your skin between your neck and your waist. I am crying because I love you so much. My tears fall on you and are warm on your scars.

When you drink too much I will beat you.

When I drink too much I will beat you.

Now we can have a baby. I am you and you are me. Out of the fire between us comes the baby.

The fire is in the kitchen, its flames leaping high. The mother is in the kitchen, tending the fire and the baby.

I can come into the kitchen to warm myself at the fire as often as I want, and the mother will never turn me away.

After I am married I shall keep coming back to the kitchen, to warm myself at her red hands.

Look in the mirror, the mother says, and see how beautiful you are. Silly, you're holding the mirror in the wrong place. Hold it lower down. See the red fire glowing there, in the secret place between your legs. See how beautiful you are. You are like me. You are my daughter. I will love you for ever. You can leave me and you can always come back.

I have branded you with the mark of my love. You are my red baby.

Out of the love between us comes the fire, and the warm kitchen, and the mother in the kitchen. Every time we make the fire, we make the kitchen, and the mother.

You can love me, and you can love your mother. You do not have to choose between us.

I shall get married in the kitchen. My mother dropped me in the fire, but she will heal me. She will heal me with her tears.

I shall love you for ever and I shall not beat you.

For my wedding I shall be dressed in red. I shall bring you my red gifts.

I threw my mother in the fire. I shall heal her. I shall heal her, with my tears.

My father and mother love each other so much. I came out of the fire between them. They marry inside me, in the red kitchen.

I take you inside me. I am not afraid of the fire any more. It is inside me. I am in the kitchen. You are there and you do not beat me.

Guillaume found he missed his daughter once she was married to Pierre and living down at the bottom of the hill in the schoolhouse. She did not come to Mass and so he never saw her in church. Sometimes on Sundays she walked along the village street with her husband, but she had little enough to say to her parents if she met them. Pierre kept a tight hold on her arm, and Guillaume did not know how to ask her the questions that longed to tumble out of his mouth. He thought perhaps the potato brandy had withered his tongue. The words burned his lips, then died. Sometimes Melusine climbed up the hill to visit her old home, but she sat by the fire in the kitchen gossiping to her stepmother and Guillaume was plainly in the way. Women's talk. He could not enter it, had never known how to. Sometimes he took her little gifts, a basket of eggs or a bunch of freshly picked rosemary or a calf's foot, and she would thank him with a nod and go back to her housework. The words he could not speak swelled in his throat and made it sore.

When Guillaume heard that Melusine was staying longer and longer each month in the pantry, he was persuaded by Madame Tarentin to go down and have a word with her. What word? He knew, but could not say it. She sat silent in front of his silence, and he went away again.

He drank at the bar less than he used to. He stayed at home with his wife and drank potato brandy in the kitchen, Madame Tarentin sitting close by him. They had begun to have a secret. Neither of them spoke of it to the other, but they read of it in each other's eyes. What was happening to Melusine? Would she go the same way as her mother?

On the night of the full moon in November of the year that Melusine disappeared, Guillaume crept out of his bed, down the hill and into the village. He stood underneath the schoolhouse pantry window and tapped at the closed shutters. No chink of light showed, but he knew his daughter was in there. His heart reached through all obstacles, knocking so loudly he knew Melusine must hear it.

She opened the windows, then the shutters, and leaned out in a swift glad movement, her eyes bright, a smile on her lips, her hands coming up in welcome. When she saw her father she drew back, all her delight falling off her like an old shawl.

– Oh, she said: it's you.

Guillaume reached up his hand and patted her arm. She frowned.

– Melusine, he pleaded, making an effort to get the words out of his burning mouth: please let me talk to you.

– Go away, she hissed.

She was dressed only in her nightgown. Tiny pleats flowed from the worn linen yoke. He reached his hands out and tore open the front of the nightgown, then clutched the folds of white linen so that she could not jerk back and escape from him. He saw the red skin, puckered and shiny and ridged, the scars as angry as though she had been dropped in the fire that very day.

– My daughter, he whispered.

Melusine shut her eyes, and turned her head away.

Then Guillaume wept. His tears fell on the scarred skin around his daugher's breasts and flowed on to his hands, warm and stinging. He could not see for weeping. So they remained at the window, the daughter and the father, knotted together by the nightgown, while Guillaume cried.

When he opened his eyes at last, he saw that the skin on his daughter's breast was as creamy and smooth as it had been on the day she was born, and that there was no blemish anywhere on her.

Footnote: I should like to acknowledge, with gratitude, the inspiration of the work of Toni Morrison.

God's House

Inside the priest's house it was very dark. I flattened my palms against the invisible air then advanced step by tiptoeing step. I smelt dust and the dregs of wine. I'd left the heat outside. The curved edge of a stone doorway was cold, grazed my cheek. Groping forwards, I encountered glass, a metal catch. With a rattle and squeak of iron bars I undid the shutters, pushed them open. Light drowned me. I saw that I was in a kitchen, bare except for a cooker and oilcloth-covered table. Sunlight fell across glistening brown paint on to my hands. I turned around and leaned back against the windowsill.

I was a burglar. My first break and entry. I wasn't sure what I wanted to steal.

I was back with you, in our old house where I'd been born twelve years before. Now a veranda had been added on at the front, bellying forwards into the garden, and your bed had been put there under the dome of glass. Half in and half out. You sat up when you saw me come in, and held out your arms.

– You haven't left yet then, I said.

The room behind us was full of relatives, a sort of party going on. You gestured towards me to come closer. You held all my attention: your lashless monkey eyes that were very bright, your translucent skin, your full, blistered lips, the outline of your head under its fuzz of curls. Everything that there was between us concentrated into that look we exchanged. Above the glass roof was the red sky, the break of dawn.

For a while the road ran through the plain, along the poplar-lined Canal du Midi, and then it rose, as the land lifted itself and became hillier. A straight road, running between golden-green plane trees, towards Spain. The rounded hills, brown and dark yellow, took us up, and up. We swung off the main road on to a smaller one, and one yet smaller.

Our village was called Beauregard-du-Perdu. We turned, as instructed, by the wash-house and fountain, and drove up the main street lined with plane trees. A green tunnel pierced with bits of dancing light. At its top I saw the stone bulk of the church, a rounded doorway decorated with zigzags. To the right, behind low gates of grey metal, was the house my aunt and uncle were renting from some French friends. We recognised it straight away from the photographs. I got out of the car and saw the other house, opposite. No. What I saw was the high wall enclosing it, the steps up to the padlocked wooden door in the wall, worn steps that curved sideways then went up to the church 35 behind. A notice tacked to the door, just above the padlock, said A VENDRE. As I stared, the church bells began to clang out the hour and I started back from their dull, flat noise.

My aunt bent towards me.

– Lily. Would you like to be the one to knock on the neighbour's door and ask for the keys? Show us how well you speak French.

I inspected the gravel under my new shoes that I'd bought for the funeral. The gravel was grey like the metal gates, loose chips under my stiff toes. I lifted a foot and scraped it along the ground.

– No point, my uncle said: here she is anyway.

Our letter of introduction named her as Madame Cabazou, a widow. She came out of the alleyway opposite our house, below the wall with its wooden door and its FOR SALE notice. A blue enamel sign proclaimed that the alley was called Impasse des Saints. Madame Cabazou was as quick as one of the lizards on the hot wall nearby. Small and skinny, eyes black as olives in her brown face, grey hair cut short. Gold daisies in her pierced ears. Her marriage earrings, she told me later on: that she wore every day. Flick flick went her tongue in her mouth as she exclaimed and shook hands and pulled the key from her housecoat pocket and ushered us in. She darted off again with a wave of her hand, a promise to bring us a bowl of plums picked that morning from the trees in her field.

Our holiday home was a little house on three floors, its walls painted a cool blue-grey. Red speckled tiles underfoot downstairs, unpolished wooden floorboards in the two bedrooms. Up here the windows had white shutters that creased up like concertinas and let in long arms of brambles laden with roses, and tiny balconies, no bigger than windowsills, in white-painted wrought iron. The bed in my room was narrow and high, with a white cover. The chairs were old-fashioned, with curvy backs. They broke when you sat on them; they were just for show.

The garden was large considering it was in the middle of a village, my aunt said. It was mainly grass, with flower-beds and tangly shrubs dotted about in it. The solid privet hedge surrounding it was such a dark green it was almost black. Over it reared the plane trees that lined the village street outside. Sage green, almond green, sea green, bottle green, those were the colours of the bushes and plants. The flowers were so bright with the light in them, mauve and pink. The sun dazzling down on the garden at midday made it white. Too hot to sit in without a hat. I felt scorched. I preferred the coolness of the broken-down barn with its earth floor, where swallows flashed in and out, quick blue streaks. On the first morning the swallows flew into my room when I was still in bed and I felt welcomed.

I was puzzled when the telephone rang. I hadn't seen one the night before. There it was, by the bed. I lifted the receiver and said hello.

Your voice sounded exactly as it always did.

– Hello, you said back to me: how are you getting on?

– D'you mean to say, I asked: that they've got telephones up there?

You laughed.

– Of course we have. How else could we get in touch? Now come on, I haven't much time, how's your father managing, and how are you?

– Oh he's doing fine, I said: more or less. You know. He's being extra careful when he drives the car.

Why did I say that? I don't know. Just then the church bells began to ring, battering the windowpanes, and your voice faded away under their onslaught.

My aunt and uncle were welded to their white plastic lounging chairs. Turned towards each other, they held hands and chatted. They were pink-faced, melting in the heat. I strolled past them with a wave, went out to explore the village.

The church door seemed locked. I shoved it with my shoulder but its resistance didn't yield. I wandered on past it, paused at an open pair of tall wrought-iron gates, went in.

I was in the cemetery. The village within the village. The houses of the dead neatly arranged side by side. The path ran all the way round, tombs on both sides. Some of the graves were just mounds of earth, with fragile, blackened crosses in crumbling iron at their heads. Others were doors laid down on the ground, thick polished stone bearing pots of pink and red porcelain roses, open porcelain books with gilt letters spelling out the names of the dead. Whole families seemed to be crammed into small tight plots. Some of the graves had photographs in black metal frames. Some had stone angels. One had a crucifix made of tiny black beads.

Madame Cabazou knelt by a shiny slab of white granite. She inserted mauve flowers, like the ones in our garden, into a black vase on top of it. I looked over her shoulder to read her husband's name carved into the stone. Emile.

– He died three months ago, Madame Cabazou said: I'm not used to it yet.

She stood up and clasped my arm. Then she held my hand in hers. Water shone in her eyes, tipped over, flowed down her cheeks.

Just behind the graves the hills began, high and round, crusted with yellow sunflowers. The landscape crackled with their dark gold and black. The earth was a rich brown. We were high up in a wild and lonely place. From here you could see the Pyrenees, misty blue shapes against the blue sky.

Madame Cabazou wore a black housecoat printed with pink roses. She let go of me and fished a handkerchief out of her pocket. She mopped her eyes.

– The village is dying, she said: we used to have vineyards up there but not any more. Only sunflowers now round here. So all the young ones have gone. Just us old people left. It's good your family has come to stay. You'll liven us up.

– They're not my parents, I told her: they're my uncle and 39 aunt.

Madame Cabazou whistled. An ancient beagle bitch trundled out of the bushes, panting, and followed us down the path. I winced away from her in case she snapped or bit.

– Betty, Betty, good dog, said Madame Cabazou: oh she's a good dog my Betty, all the dogs in the village are good, none of them will harm you, they don't bite.

– My mother's just died, I said in the loudest voice I could manage: so they've brought me away on holiday to be nice to me.

Madame Cabazou stood stock still in the centre of the path and cried some more.

– Oh poor child poor child poor little one.

She hung on to my hand again as she wept. Then she blew her nose and shut the tall gates behind us. The church bells began to clamour out the Angelus. Bash, bash, bash.

– Electronic, said Madame Cabazou: the old lady who used to ring the Angelus, because her father did before her, she died this spring. No village priest any longer, either. Just one who serves all the villages in turn. The presbytery's been empty for a long time.

She fingered the little silver crucifix slung round her neck on a silver chain and sighed.

– The presbytery? I asked.

– The priest's house, she said: there.

We were going down the stone steps from the side of the church, down into the well of green light under the plane trees. She waved her hand at the high wall beside us, the wooden door let into it. We paused there, on the corner of the alleyway, to say goodbye.

– Oh this heat, she said: I do love it. And it's so good for my arthritis.

She tapped me on the cheek.

– You must have faith. Your mother is with God. We must believe that. She's up there in heaven. She's alive for all eternity.

She hurried off. The old dog lurched along after her, slack-bellied, velvety nose in the dust.

You grasped my hand. We took off together with a swift kick, we whirred into the night sky. Holding on to you I was drawn along, buoyant, an effortless progress under the stars above the wheeling earth.

We flew into the mouth of a dark tunnel. I could see nothing, I gripped your hand, felt cold air stream over my eyelids. You knew your way. You carried us both along, our arms were wings.

– I wanted to show you what dying was like, you said: I wanted you to know. Open your eyes. Look.

Below us, in the tunnel, were hospital beds crowded with sick people. They lay still and silent, faces upturned as we flew past. Then they dwindled behind us, and we burst out of the tunnel back into the soft blackness of the night.

– That was dying, you said: we've gone past death now.

Our curving flight traced the shape of the earth below. We swooped sideways, down. Another opening loomed. 41

Another tunnel? I wasn't sure. The silvery stars rolled past. We were carried on the shoulders of the wind.

– There's a lot more I've got to find out about, you explained: I've got a lot more to explore. Come on, let's go in here next.

A mosquito whined in my ear. I cursed and sat up. You were no longer there.

We ate lunch in the garden, beside the hedge, under the shade of a big white umbrella. Onion tart and tomato salad, bread and cheese, a plate of dark blue figs. My aunt and uncle drank a lot of wine. They went indoors for a siesta.

I sat on, idly looking at the bushes, the flowerbeds. All sun-drenched, glittering. The shutters of the rooms upstairs were only half closed. I heard my aunt call out and laugh. Her noise rattled against my skin.

The dog Betty appeared in the farthest corner of the garden. She emerged from under the fig tree which grew there, began to toddle across the grass. She pursued her sedate, determined way as though it were marked out for her, pushing aside tall clumps of weeds that blocked her path, stepping delicately over the empty wine bottle my uncle had let fall. She didn't bother looking at me. I decided she must be on some private dog-road, some sort of dogs' short-cut via holes in our hedge we hadn't seen.

She flattened herself by the gate and tried to wriggle under. She was too fat to manage it. She whined and thumpped her tail. I got up and opened the gate. She trotted through, then paused. She was waiting for me. I thought I would follow her to find out where she'd go.

She crossed the road and turned into the alley. Madame Cabazou's house, I knew, was the first one along. On the opposite side, on the corner with the street, was the priest's house behind its high wall. Betty didn't go home to her mistress. She nosed at a low wicker gate set into the wall near the end of the alley.

I tore aside the rusty wire netting stretched across the top of the gate and peered over it. A short path, overhung with creepers, led steeply upwards to a stone façade half obscured by leaves. I understood. This was a back way into the priest's house, one not protected by padlocks and keys. In a moment I'd climbed through the netting and over the gate and dropped down on the other side. The branches of trees brushed my face and arms. Soft debris of dead leaves under my feet. I stood still and listened. The entire village seemed to be asleep. No sharp voice, no tap on my shoulder, pulled me back. I crept up the path. I forgot Betty: she'd gone.

The house rose up before me, wide, three solid storeys of cream-coloured stone under a red-tiled roof. Blank-faced, its brown shutters closed. Three steps led up to its double wooden door. On either side of this were stone benches with claw feet; and tall bushes of oleander spilling worn pink flowers along the ground. I didn't hurry working out how to enter the house because the garden laid insistent hands on me and made me want to stay in it for ever.

From the outside you couldn't see that there was a garden at all. It was hidden. A secret place. It was small and square and overgrown, completely enclosed by the towering walls that surrounded it: the house on one side, the neighbour's barn on a second, and the walls of the street and the alleyway on the other two.

Inside these walls the garden was further enclosed by a luxuriant green vine trained on to wires. What must once have been a tidy green plot edged by the vine, by bushes and trees, was now a thicket you had to push your way into. I crept into a little sweet-smelling box of wilderness. Just big enough to hold me. Just the right size. In its green heart I stood upright in the long grass and counted two cherry trees, an apple tree laden with fruit, more oleanders, a lofty bush of bamboo plumes and several of blackcurrant. I picked a leaf and rubbed it to release the harsh scent. There was an ancient well in one corner, fenced about with cobwebs and black iron spikes. I lifted its wooden lid, peered down at its black mirror, threw a pebble in and heard the far splash.

I was frightened of going into the house all by myself, so I dared myself to do it as soon as the church bells began to strike the hour. The doors were clasped together merely by a loop of thin wire. I twisted a stick in it, broke it. Then I pushed the doors open and entered the house.

Once I'd wrestled with the shutters in the kitchen and flung them wide, screeching on their unoiled hinges, I could see. The red-tiled floor, the white fireplace with columns on either side and a white carving of scrolls and flowers above, the stone arch I'd come through from the hall, the cooker black with grease, the yellow oilcloth on the table.

A corridor wound around the ground floor. I passed a store-room full of old furniture and carpentry things, a wine cellar lined with empty metal racks, a poky lavatory with decorated blue tiles going up the wall. I picked my way up an open wooden staircase, like a ladder, to the salon and the bedrooms above. The salon was empty, grand as a ballroom but desolate. Striped blue and gold wallpaper hung down in curly strips, exposing the plaster and laths behind. The floor was bendy when I walked on it. The bedrooms were dusty and dark, falls of soot piled in their fireplaces. Old stained mattresses rested on broken-down springs, old books, parched covers stiff with dirt, sprawled face down on the lino, old chairs with cracked backs and seats were mixed up anyhow with rolls of lino, split satin cushions.

I put out my hands and touched these things in the half-dark. I draped my shoulders with a torn bedspread of scarlet chenille, then passed my hands over the wounded furniture. I blessed it, I told it to be healed now, and that it was forgiven. Then I departed from those sad rooms, closing their doors behind me one by one.

I crawled up a second wooden stair, to the attic. Bright spears of light tore gaps in the walls and roof, pointed at a floor littered with feathers and droppings. A headless plaster statue leaned in the far corner. His hands clasped a 45 missal. He wore a surplice and cassock. I recognised him, even without his head, as St John Vianney, the curé of Ars. We'd done him at school. I looked for his head among the dusty junk surrounding him but couldn't find it. So I went back downstairs, into the garden again.

My bed in our old house was in the corner of the room. Shadows fingered the wall next to me and lay down on me like blankets. You'd draped a shadow over your face like a mantilla. You advanced, carrying a night-light. I was afraid of the dark but not of you, even though a grey cobwebby mask clung to your eyes and mouth and hid them.

You bent over me and spoke.

– What a mess you've left everything in. Bits and pieces all over the place. Silly girl.

You whispered in my ear.

– One day I'll tell you all the secrets I've ever known.

My aunt ladled cold cucumber soup from the white china tureen into white soup plates. We pushed our spoons across the pale green ponds, to and fro like swimmers. My spoon was big, silver-plated; I liked its heaviness in my hand. My uncle drank his soup heartily, stuffed in mouthfuls of bread, called for a second helping. My aunt waved the ladle at the moths butting the glass dome of the lamp she'd set on the table. It threw just enough light for us to eat by. The rest of the garden was swallowed by black night. From Madame Cabazou's house across the street came the sound of a man's voice reading the news on TV.

My aunt and uncle spoke to each other and left me in peace. I could lean against their chat like a pillow while I searched my memory.

– No, my father said on the morning of the funeral: I don't believe in the afterlife. Though your mother tried to. Bound to, wasn't she, being a Catholic. We just conk out I think. That's the end of it. The end of consciousness.

My uncle's red cheeks bulged with bread. He caught my eye and lifted his glass to me. My aunt collected our empty soup plates and stacked them on one side of the table. My uncle swallowed his faceful of bread and fetched the next course. Stuffed red peppers. I lifted mine out of the dish on to my plate, inserted my knife, slit the red skin. The pepper fell apart easily, like a bag of thin red silk. Rice and mushrooms tumbled out, a strip of anchovy.

– Overcooked, frowned my aunt: your fault, Lily, for coming back so late. Whatever were you up to?

I shrugged and smiled.

– Oh we understand, she said: you're young, you don't want to hang around all the time with us middle-aged folks! And we trust you to be sensible. Not to do anything silly.

She began to toss green salad in a clear plastic bowl, moving the wooden spoons delicately between the oily leaves that gave off the fragrance of tarragon.

– Of course you need some time by yourself, she said: especially just now. You want to amuse yourself, spend time by yourself, that's fine. Of course we understand.

It was early evening when I arrived at the house. Climbing the hill had taken me several hours. Now the sky at the horizon was green, as sharp as apples. The moon rose. A single silver star burned high above the lavender-blue sea.

The house was built into the cliff, at the very top, where the chalky ground levelled out, became turf dotted with gorse, sea-pinks, scabious. The front door stood open so I went in.

The whole place smelt of freshly sawn wood. Fragrance of resin, of cedar. Large rooms, airy and light. The walls and ceilings were painted a clear glowing blue. Beds were dotted about, manuscripts spilled across them. I wondered who they were, the people who lived here and strewed their papers over their beds. Then I saw the figure of a woman in the far doorway, leaning against the frame of the door, with her back to me. The owner of the house. Would she mind my presence? I was uninvited. A trespasser.

She turned round.

I'd forgotten that you'd ever looked like this. Young, with thick curly brown hair, amused hazel eyes, fresh unlined skin. Not a trace of sorrow or of pain. You were healthy. You were fully alive.

– I'm living here now, you explained with a smile and a wave of the hand: in Brahma's house.

You walked me about the spacious blue rooms, up and down the wide, ladder-like staircases of golden wood.

– Tell your father, you said: the cure for grief is, you have to sit by an open window and look out of it.

Your face was calm. No fear in it. You weren't suffering any more.

– You look so well, I blurted out: and all your hair's grown back!

– It's time for you to go, you told me.

You stood on the front steps and waved me off. My eyes measured the width of the doorway. I thought I'd slip through, stay with you. You shook your head, slammed the door shut on my efforts to break back in.

At eight o'clock prompt each day a siren wailed along the main road. That second morning, Madame Cabazou leaned over our gates and called.

– The bread van. Hurry up, girl. It doesn't wait long.

I stumbled after her, half-asleep. She dashed along on nimble slippered feet, a thick cardigan thrust on over her white nightdress. The dog Betty trailed us, folds of fat swaying.

Down by the fountain we joined a queue of old people who all smiled and exclaimed. Madame Cabazou introduced me, made me shake hands all round. Once I was part of them they went on swapping bits of news. Madame Cabazou was the lively one. Her chatter was staccato, her hands flew about like the swallows that zigzagged between our house and barn.

– My wretched grandchildren, she cried: they hardly ever come and see me. Children these days. Oh they don't care.

I bought a bag of croissants and a thick loaf, one up from

a baguette, that was called simply a *pain*. I walked slowly back up the street to the house. The voices of the old people rose and fell behind me, bubbles of sound, like the splash of water in the fountain. They were recalling the funeral they'd been to the week before. A young girl, from a farm over by the lake, had been trapped by her hair in her father's baling machine and strangled. The voices grew high and excited, like the worrying of dogs.

After breakfast my aunt and uncle drove off in the car to visit the castle at Montsegur. I waved them goodbye, then prowled about the kitchen, collecting the things I needed and packing them into a basket. I shut the grey metal gates behind me and crossed the road into the alleyway.

Madame Cabazou was working in the little vegetable patch in front of her house. Her thin body was bent double as she tugged weeds from the earth. Today she had on a blue housecoat, and she'd tied her straw hat on like a bonnet, the strings knotted under her chin. I slunk past while her stooped back was turned and hoisted myself over the wicker gate.

Once inside the priest's kitchen I opened the shutters and the windows to let in light and air. I swept the floor with the dustpan and brush I'd brought, dusted the table and the fireplace and the windowsills. I laid a fire, with sticks and bits of wood from the store-room. I'd brought a small saucepan to cook in. I had a metal fish-slice and one wooden spoon. For lunch I might have stewed apples, using the fruit from the tree outside. I might try mixing up some grape juice. I had three plastic bottles of mineral water in my basket, a croissant saved from breakfast, a blue and white checked teacloth, and a couple of books. I left all this equipment on the table in the kitchen, and went outside.

I dropped into the garden like a stone or a plant, taking up my place. The garden had been waiting for me. I belonged in it. I had discovered it and in that act had been accepted by it. Now I was part of it. Hidden, invisible. The long grass closed over my head, green water. The bushes stretched wide their flowering branches around me. The bright green vine walled me in with its jagged leaves, curling tendrils, heavy bunches of grapes. Around the edges of the garden rustled the tops of the trees.

I had plenty of time to get to know the garden. I had seven whole days in which to stare at the ants and beetles balanced on the blades of grass next to my face, to finger the different textures of stems, to listen to the crickets and birds. I rolled over on to my back, put my hands under my head, and stared at the sky through branches and leaves. My hammock. I swung in it upside down. It dandled me. I fell asleep and didn't wake for hours.

Over supper my aunt and uncle told me about the castle of Montsegur, perched on top of a steep mountain. They'd climbed up the slippery rocks. They'd eaten their picnic in the lofty stronghold where the Cathars had held out against St Dominic's armies come to smash them and drag them down to the waiting pyre.

– God how I loathe the Catholic Church, cried my aunt:

God how I loathe all priests!

My uncle poured red wine into tumblers.

– Nice day, Lily? he asked.

I nodded. My mouth was full of cream-laden spaghetti scented with rosemary and sage. I had the idea that if I kept on eating the memory of my mother wouldn't be able to climb out of my silence, out of the long gaps between my words, and disturb me. So I held out my plate for a second helping and bent my head over. I concentrated on the pleasures of biting, of chewing and swallowing, the pleasure of feeling full.

I was in bed but I wasn't asleep. The room was dark, and very warm. Gold glow of a lamp in one corner. Rain beat against the window, I heard it shush-shush through the curtains. Around me was folded the softest and lightest of quilts. Like being tucked up in a cloud. Or held in your arms. For you were there, a dim presence by the lamp, humming to yourself while you read a book about gardening. Peace was the physical knowledge of warmth, of your familiar profile, your sleeve of dark pink silk resting on the plump arm of your chair, the dim blue and gold pattern of the wallpaper.

You repeated to me: you're safe now. Safe now. Safe now.

– Our last day, Lily, smiled my aunt: are you sure you don't want to come out with us for a drive? I can't think what you find to do on your own here day after day.

I shook my head.

– Well, she said: if you don't, you don't, I suppose. You could make a start on your packing, in that case.

Her words jolted me. For seven days I'd been in retreat, in my private green world. I'd ceased to hear the church bells banging out the hours overhead. Hunger was my only clock. A week, in which I'd laid on the grass reading or daydreaming, had flowed past without my knowing or caring what day it was. Back home my schoolbooks waited, and a timetable ruled into squares.

I had an ache inside me. A sort of yawn that hurt. A voice in my stomach that wanted to scream. I felt stretched, and that I might topple over and break in two.

Back home I'd enter an empty house. My mother was dead. If only that could be a fact that was well past, something I'd dealt with and got over. Recovered from. I didn't want to embark on a life in which she'd go on and on being dead, on and on not being there. I didn't want to let it catch up with me. I shut the grey metal gates and hurried across the road.

Madame Cabazou was sitting on her front step, picking fleas out of Betty's coat. She nipped them between her fingernails until their little black backs cracked. Crack! Crack! She brushed the fleas from her fingertips like grains of black sand.

– Do you want some melons? she asked: I've got far too many. Even with this tiny patch I've grown more, this year, than I can use.

She waved her hand at the tidy rows of tomatoes, melons and courgettes. The earth between them was spotless, fine as sieved flour. She scowled at it.

– We used to have proper fields of crops, and the vineyard. Not like this. This pocket handkerchief of a garden. Oh I do miss all that, I can't tell you how much.

– Perhaps one melon? I suggested: we're leaving tomorrow morning early. We could have melon tonight.

– Come and fetch it later on, she sang out: I'll pick you one that's really ripe.

She shoved Betty's nose off her lap, and got up. She put her hands in her pockets and gazed at me.

She jerked her head towards the wicker gate in the wall.

– Some German people coming to view the house this afternoon, she remarked: with a lady from the agency.

I tried to sound indifferent.

– Oh really?

– The man who drives the bread-van told me, she said: this morning. His brother-in-law works in the café next door to the agency in Carcassonne, he heard them talking about it when they came in for a beer. Didn't you hear him say so down at the van this morning? You were off in some dream.

Coldness clutched me inside. I stared at Madame Cabazou.

– If I were you, she said: I'd come and fetch that melon this afternoon. You dream too much, it's not good. Better wake up. Otherwise you can be sure you'll be in trouble.

Too much time by yourself, that's your problem.

Her words hurt me like slaps on the face. I swung away without saying anything. Tears burned my eyes but I wouldn't cry while she was watching me. I heard her front door close, then her voice drifted through the window, scolding Betty, breaking into song. She was cold-hearted. She didn't care how much she'd upset me. She didn't know how it felt to be told I'd got to leave this house and this garden for good.

I'd believed for a whole week that it was my house, my garden. I'd hardly believed it even. I just knew it. I'd just been part of it. The garden had seemed to know me, had taken me in without fuss. Leaving it, going outside and not coming back, would be like having my skin peeled off. I might die. Something was tearing me apart inside. It frightened me. I was a piece of paper being slowly ripped in two. I staggered, and fell on to the little patch of tangled grass under the vine. I started crying and could not stop. The crying went on and on, and the pain. It twisted me up, it sawed me, it squeezed my heart so I could hardly breathe. The worst thing was feeling so lonely, and knowing I always would.

Just before my mother died, the night before, I was with her. It wasn't her any more, this tiny person so thin under her nightie I couldn't bear to look at her, with clawlike hands and a head that was a skull. Her eyes were the same, that was the only part of her left that I knew. She looked out of the darkness she was in and recognised me. For a couple of minutes she fought her way up from the morphine and tried to speak. She looked at me so trustfully. My father had said I should say goodbye to her but I couldn't.

– You're not going to die just yet are you, I said loudly: you're not going to die just yet.

Her cracked lips tried to smile.

– Oh yes I am, she whispered: oh yes I think I am.

That night I dreamed of her bed in the glass conservatory, half in and half out of the house. I woke up at dawn and saw the sky like red glass. My father came in and said my mother had just died.

I could think of her being alive. I could think of her being dead. What I could not bear to think of was that moment when she died, was dying, died. When she crossed over from being alive to being dead. I couldn't join the two things up, I couldn't connect them, because at the point where they met and changed into each other was pain, my body caught in a vice, my bones twisted and wrenched, my guts torn apart. I gave birth to her dying. Violently she was pulled out of me. I felt I was dying too. I could hear an animal howling. It was me.

I lay on the grass exhausted. I felt empty. Nothing left in me. I was an old sack used then thrown away. Now I was low as the grass, low as the ground. Flattened. I was worn out. As though a mountain had stamped on me.

A yawn possessed me and I looked up. My eyelids felt swollen like car tyres, and my nose too, and my mouth. I licked the salt tears off the corners of my lips, blew my nose.

I lay staring at the gnarled trunk of the vine, the weeds and grasses stirring about its root, the yellow flowers mixed in with them whose name I didn't know.

Then it stopped being me looking at the vine, because I dissolved into it, became it. I left me behind. Human was the same as plant. This corner of the garden, the earth: one great warm breathing body that was all of us, that lived strongly, whose life I felt coursing inside me, sap blood juices of grass. Love was the force that made things grow. Love grew the vine, the weeds, me. I started crying again because of the joy. It swept through me. The knowledge of love. Such sweetness and warmth inside me and the vine and the grass under the light of the sun.

Madame Cabazou whistled for me as though I were Betty. We both came running. I carried a melon home under each arm. She kissed me on both cheeks to say goodbye, instructed me, if I wished to be well thought of, to write to her. She snatched me out of my garden, shook me, set me upright, told me to go home now. She pushed me off.

Next morning I slumped in the back seat of the car as we drove out of the village and headed for the motorway. I wanted to take the road back, to go the other way, to stay. I cried as we left the high golden hills and descended on to the plain. The wind from the sea, that Madame Cabazou called the *marin*, blew strongly. It meant the end of summer. It sang an elegy for my mother. She was dead she was gone I had lost her she would never come back and live with us again.

Every cell in every leaf had had a voice, which spoke to me.

– *Of course I am here. Where else should I be but here. Where else could I possibly be.*

A Note on Michèle Roberts

Half-English and half-French, Michèle Roberts was born in 1949. Her permanent home is London. She is the author of seven highly acclaimed novels, including *Daughters of the House*, shortlisted for the Booker Prize and winner of the W.H. Smith Literary Award, and *Flesh and Blood*. Author of three solo collections of poetry, Michèle Roberts has also co-authored four volumes of short stories.